LOVE
THAT
DOG

ALSO BY SHARON CREECH

WALK TWO MOONS
ABSOLUTELY NORMAL CHAOS
PLEASING THE GHOST
CHASING REDBIRD
BLOOMABILITY
THE WANDERER
FISHING IN THE AIR
A FINE, FINE SCHOOL

SHARON CREECH

LOVE
THAT
DOG

SCHOLASTIC INC.
New York Toronto London Auckland Sydney
Mexico City New Delhi Hong Kong Buenos Aires

JACK

SEPTEMBER 13

I don't want to
because boys
don't write poetry.

Girls do.

SEPTEMBER 21

I tried.
Can't do it.
Brain's empty.

September 27

I don't understand
the poem about
the red wheelbarrow
and the white chickens
and why so much
depends upon
them.

If that is a poem
about the red wheelbarrow
and the white chickens
then any words
can be a poem.
You've just got to
make
short
lines.

OCTOBER 4

Do you promise
not to read it
out loud?
Do you promise
not to put it
on the board?

Okay, here it is,
but I don't like it.

> *So much depends*
> *upon*
> *a blue car*
> *splattered with mud*
> *speeding down the road.*

OCTOBER 10

What do you mean—
*Why does so much depend
upon
a blue car?*

You didn't say before
that I had to tell *why*.

The wheelbarrow guy
didn't tell *why*.

OCTOBER 17

What was up with
the snowy woods poem
you read today?

Why doesn't the person just
keep going if he's got
so many miles to go
before he sleeps?

And why do I have to tell more
about the blue car
splattered with mud
speeding down the road?

I don't want to
write about that blue car
that had miles to go
before it slept,
so many miles to go
in such a hurry.

OCTOBER 24

I am sorry to say
I did not really understand
the tiger tiger burning bright poem
but at least it sounded good
in my ears.

Here is the blue car
with tiger sounds:

*Blue car, blue car, shining bright
in the darkness of the night:
who could see you speeding by
like a comet in the sky?*

*I could see you in the night,
blue car, blue car, shining bright.
I could see you speeding by
like a comet in the sky.*

Some of the tiger sounds
are still in my ears
like drums
beat-beat-beating.

OCTOBER 31

Yes
you can put
the two blue-car poems
on the board
but only if
you don't put
my name
on them.

NOVEMBER 6

They look nice
typed up like that
on blue paper
on a yellow board.

(But still don't tell anyone
who wrote them, okay?)

(And what does *anonymous* mean?
Is it good?)

November 9

I don't have any pets
so I can't write about one
and especially
I can't write
a POEM
about one.

November 15

Yes, I used to have a pet.
I don't want to write about it.

You're going to ask me
Why not?
Right?

Pretend I still have that pet?

Can't I make up a pet—
a different one?
Like a tiger?
Or a hamster?
A goldfish?
Turtle?
Snail?
Worm?
Flea?

NOVEMBER 29

I liked those
small poems
we read today.

When they're small
like that
you can read
a whole bunch
in a short time
and then in your head
are all the pictures
of all the small things
from all the small poems.

I liked how the kitten leaped
in the cat poem
and how you could see
the long head of the horse
in the horse poem

and especially I liked the dog
in the dog poem
because that's just how
my yellow dog
used to lie down,
with his tongue all limp
and his chin
between
his paws
and how he'd sometimes
chomp at a fly
and then sleep
in his loose skin,
just like that poet,
Miss Valerie Worth,
says,
in her small
dog poem.

December 4

Why do you want
to type up what I wrote
about reading
the small poems?

It's not a poem.
Is it?

I guess you can
put it on the board
if you want to
but don't put
my name
on it
in case
other people
think
it's not a poem.

December 13

I guess it does
look like a poem
when you see it
typed up
like that.

But I think maybe
it would look better
if there was more space
between the lines.
Like how I wrote it
the first time.

And I liked the picture
of the yellow dog
you put beside it.

But that's not how
my yellow dog
looked.

January 10

I really really really
did NOT get
the pasture poem
you read today.

I mean:
somebody's going out
to the pasture
to clean the spring
and to get
the little tottery calf
while he's out there
and he isn't going
to be gone long
and he wants YOU
(who is YOU?)
to come too.

I mean REALLY.

And you said that
Mr. Robert Frost
who wrote
about the pasture
was also the one
who wrote about
those snowy woods
and the miles to go
before he sleeps—
well!

I think Mr. Robert Frost
has a little
too
much
time
on his
hands.

JANUARY 17

Remember the wheelbarrow poem
you read
the first week
of school?

Maybe the wheelbarrow poet
was just
making a picture
with words
and
someone else—
like maybe his teacher—
typed it up
and then people thought
it was a poem
because
it looked like one
typed up like that.

And maybe
that's the same thing
that happened with
Mr. Robert Frost.
Maybe he was just
making pictures with words
about the snowy woods
and the pasture—
and his teacher
typed them up
and they *looked* like poems
so people thought
they were poems.

Like how you did
with the blue-car things
and reading-the-small-poems thing.
On the board

typed up
they look like
poems
and the other kids
are looking at them
and they think
they really are
poems
and they
are all saying
Who wrote that?

We were going for a drive
and my father said
We won't be gone long—
You come too
and so I went
and we drove and drove
until we stopped at a
red brick building
with a sign
in blue letters
ANIMAL PROTECTION SHELTER.

And inside we walked
down a long cement path
past cages
with all kinds of
dogs
big and small
fat and skinny

some of them
hiding in the corner
but most of them
bark-bark-barking and
jumping up
against the wire cage
as we walked past
as if they were saying
Me! Me! Choose me!
I'm the best one!

And that's where we saw
the yellow dog
standing against the cage
with his paws curled
around the wire
and his long red tongue
hanging out
and his big black eyes
looking a little sad
and his long tail

wag-wag-wagging
as if he were saying
Me me me! Choose me!

And we did.
We chose him.

And in the car
he put his head
against my chest
and wrapped his paws
around my arm
as if he were saying
Thank you thank you thank you.

And the other dogs
in the cages
get killed dead
if nobody chooses them.

January 31

Yes
you can type up
what I wrote
about my yellow dog
but leave off the part
about the other dogs
getting killed dead
because that's too sad.

And don't put
my name
on it
please.

And maybe
it would look good
on yellow paper.

And maybe
the title
should be
YOU COME TOO.

FEBRUARY 7

Yes
it looks good
on yellow paper
but you forgot
(again)
to leave more
space
between the lines
like I did
when I wrote it.

That's okay though.

FEBRUARY 15

I like that poem
we read today
about street music
in the city.

My street is not
in the middle
of the city
so it doesn't have
that LOUD music
of horns and trucks
clash
flash
screech.

My street is
on the edge
of a city

and it has
quiet music
most of the time
whisp
meow
swish.

My street is a THIN one
with houses on both sides
and my house is
the white one
with the red door.

There is not too much traffic
on my street—
not like in the
middle
of a city.

We play in the yards
and sometimes

in the street
but only if
a grown-up
or the big kids
are out there, too,
and they will shout
Car!
if they see a car
coming down our street.

At both ends
of our street
are yellow signs
that say
Caution! Children at Play!
but sometimes
the cars
pay no attention
and speed down
the road
as if

they are in a BIG hurry
with many miles to go
before they sleep.

FEBRUARY 21

That was so great
those poems you showed us
where the words
make the shape
of the thing
that the poem
is about—
like the one about an apple
that was shaped like an apple
and the one about the house
that was shaped like a house.

My brain was pop-pop-popping
when I was looking at those poems.
I never knew a poet person
could do that funny
kind of thing.

FEBRUARY 26

I tried one of those
poems that looks like
what it's about.

MY YELLOW DOG
by Jack

```
                              headhead
                bodybodybody    ad        he
    tail tail    low    body        he  (EYE)  ad      sniffsniffsniff
  w   yellow yellow  body      y    E              sniffsniff
  o     y e l l     body      d  h e A d    nose
    l       o      body      o    R  head
    l         w    body    b              slobber
      e           bodybodybody
  wag                                               slobber
  wag   y        leg            leg
  wag           leg leg        leg leg
                 leg            leg              slobber
                 leg            leg
                 leg            leg
                 leg            leg
                 paw            paw
```

37

Yes
you can type up
the yellow dog poem
that looks like a dog
but this time
keep the spaces
exactly
the same
and maybe
it would look
really really good
on yellow paper.

Maybe you could
put my name on it.
But only if you want to.
Only if you think it
looks
good enough.

MARCH 7

I was
a little embarrassed
when people said
things to me like
Neat poem, Jack
and
How'd you think of that, Jack?

And I really really like
the one you put up
about the tree
that is shaped like
a tree
not a fake-looking tree
but like a real tree
with straggly branches.

But I want to know
who is the

anonymous poet
in our class
who wrote that
and why didn't
he
or
she
want to put
his or her name
on it?
Was it like me
when I didn't think
my words
were
poems?

Maybe you will tell
the anonymous tree poet
that his or her tree poem

is really
a poem
really really
and a good poem, too.

MARCH 14

That was the best best BEST
poem
you read yesterday
by Mr. Walter Dean Myers
the best best BEST
poem
ever.

I am sorry
I took the book home
without asking.
I only got
one spot
on it.
That's why
the page is torn.
I tried to get
the spot
out.

I copied that BEST poem
and hung it on my
bedroom wall
right over my bed
where I can
see it when I'm
lying
down.

Maybe you could
copy it too
and hang it
on the wall
in our class
where we can see it
when we are sitting
at our desks
doing our stuff.

I sure liked that poem
by Mr. Walter Dean Myers
called
"Love That Boy."

Because of two reasons
I liked it:
One is because
my dad calls me
in the morning
just like that.
He calls
Hey there, son!

And also because
when I had my
yellow dog
I loved that dog
and I would call him

like this—
I'd say—
Hey there, Sky!

(His name was Sky.)

MARCH 22

My yellow dog
followed me everywhere
every which way I turned
he was there
wagging his tail
and slobber
coming out
of his mouth
when he was smiling
at me
all the time
as if he was
saying
thank you thank you thank you
for choosing me
and jumping up on me
his shaggy straggly paws
on my chest
like he was trying

to hug the insides
right out of me.

And when us kids
were playing outside
kicking the ball
he'd chase after it
and push it with his nose
push push push
and getting slobber
all over the ball
but no one cared
because he was such
a funny dog
that dog Sky
that straggly furry
smiling
dog
Sky.

And I'd call him
every morning
every evening
Hey there, Sky!

MARCH 27

Yes, you can type up
what I wrote about
my dog Sky
but don't type up
that other secret one
I wrote—
the one all folded up
in the envelope
with tape on it.
That one uses too many of
Mr. Walter Dean Myers's
words
and maybe
Mr. Walter Dean Myers
would get mad
about that.

I was very glad
to hear that
Mr. Walter Dean Myers
is not the sort of person
who would get mad
at a boy
for using some of his words.

And thank you
for typing up
my secret poem
the one that uses
so many of
Mr. Walter Dean Myers's
words
and I like what
you put
at the top:
Inspired by Walter Dean Myers.

That sounds good
to my ears.
Now no one
will think
I just copied
because I
couldn't think
of my own words.
They will know
I was
inspired by
Mr. Walter Dean Myers.

But don't put it
on the board
yet, okay?

Is Mr. Walter Dean Myers
a live person?

And if he is
do you think
he could ever come
to our city
to our school
to our class?

And if he did
we should hide
my poem
with his words—
hide it real good—
just in case
he *would* get mad
about that.

No.
No, no, no, no, no.

I can't do it.

You should do it.
You're a teacher.

APRIL 12

I don't agree
that Mr. Walter Dean Myers
might like to hear
from a boy
who likes his poems.

I think Mr. Walter Dean Myers
would like to hear
from a teacher
who uses big words
and knows how
to spell
and
to type.

APRIL 17

Dear Mr. Walter Dean Myers,

You probably don't want to hear from me
because I am only a boy
and not a teacher
and I don't use
big words
and you probably won't read this
or even if you do read it
you probably are way too busy
to answer it
let alone do the thing
I am going to ask you
and I want you to know
that's okay
because our teacher says
writers are very very very very
busy
trying to write their words

and the phone is ringing
and the fax is going
and the bills need paying
and sometimes they get sick
(I hope you are not sick,
Mr. Walter Dean Myers)
or their family gets sick
or their electricity goes off
or the car needs fixing
or they have to go
to the grocery store
or do the laundry
or clean up messes.
I don't know how
you find the time
to write your words
if you have to do all that stuff
and maybe you should get
a helper.

So what I am asking you
is this:
If you ever get time
to leave your house
and if you ever feel
like visiting a school
where there might be some kids
who like your poems
would you ever maybe
think about maybe
coming
maybe
to our school
which is a clean place
with mostly nice
people in it
and I think our teacher
Miss Stretchberry
would maybe even

make brownies for you
because she sometimes
makes them for us.

I hope I haven't too much
stopped you from doing your
writing of words
and fixing your car
and getting groceries
and all that stuff—
just to read this letter
which probably is taking you
maybe fifteen minutes
and in that time
you could've maybe
written
a whole new poem
or at least the start
of one
and so I am sorry

for taking up your
time
and I understand
if you can't come
to our clean school
and read some of your poems
to us
and let us see your face
which I bet
is a friendly face.

My name is Jack.
Bye, Mr. Walter Dean Myers.

APRIL 20

Did you mail it?
Did he answer yet?

Months???
It might
take *months*
for Mr. Walter Dean Myers
to answer my letter?
If he answers it?

I didn't know—
until you explained—
that the letter has to go
to Mr. Walter Dean Myers's
publisher company
and then someone
at the publisher company
has to sort all the mail
not just my letter
but hundreds and hundreds
of letters
to hundreds of authors

all that big mess of mail
piled up
and someone sorting sorting sorting
all that mail
and then the letters for
Mr. Walter Dean Myers
go to him
and maybe he's away
maybe he's on vacation
maybe he's sick
maybe he's hiding in a room
writing poems
maybe he's baby-sitting
his children or his grandchildren
(if he's married and stuff)
or maybe he has to go
to the dentist
or get that car fixed
or maybe someone died
(I really really really hope
someone did not die)

so
if you ask me
it could take him
years
to get around
to answering
that letter
so I guess
we'd better
just forget about it
not count on it
get it out of our minds
do something else
forget it.

April 26

Sometimes
when you are trying
not to think about something
it keeps popping back
into your head
you can't help it
you think about it
and
think about it
and
think about it
until your brain
feels like
a squashed pea.

MAY 2

Yes
you can type up
the thing about
trying not to think about
something
but
you'd better
leave my name off it
because it was
just words
coming out of my head
and I wasn't paying
too much attention
to which words
came out
when.

MAY 7

Maybe you could
show me
how to use
the computer
and then
I could type up
my own words?

MAY 8

I didn't know about
the spell-checking thing
inside the computer.
It is like a miracle
little brain
in there
a little helper brain.

But I am a slow typer person.
Did you say there is
a teaching-typing thing
in that computer, too?
Will it help me type
better
and
faster
taptaptaptaptap
so my fingers
can go as fast
as my brain?

MAY 14

(I typed this up myself.)

MY SKY

We were outside
in the street
me and some other kids
kicking the ball
before dinner
and Sky was
chasing chasing chasing
with his feet going
every which way
and his tail
wag-wag-wagging
and his mouth
slob-slob-slobbering
and he was
all over the place

smiling and wagging
and slobbering
and making
us laugh
and my dad
came walking up the street
he was way down there
near the end
I could see him
after he got off the bus
and he was walk-walk-walking
and I saw him wave
and he called out
"Hey there, son!"
and so I didn't see
the car
coming from the other way
until someone else—
one of the big kids—

called out
"Car!"
and I turned around
and saw a
blue car blue car
splattered with mud
speeding down the road

And I saw Sky
going after the ball
wag-wag-wagging
his tail
and I called him
"Sky! Sky!"
and he turned his
head
but it was too late
because the
blue car blue car
splattered with mud
hit Sky

thud thud thud
and kept on going
in such a hurry
so fast
so many miles to go
it couldn't even stop
and
Sky
was just there
in the road
lying on his side
with his legs bent funny
and his side heaving
and he looked up at me
and I said
"Sky! Sky! Sky!"
and then my dad
was there
and he lifted Sky
out of the road
and laid him on the grass

and
Sky
closed his eyes
and
he
never
opened
them
again
ever.

MAY 15

I don't know.

If you put it on the board
and people read it
it might make them
sad.

Okay.
I guess.
I'll put my name on it.

But I hope it doesn't make
people feel too sad
and if it does
maybe you could
think of something
to cheer everybody up
like maybe with
some of those brownies
you make
the chocolate ones
that are so good?

MAY 21

Wow!
Wow wow wow wow wow!

That was the best best BEST
news
ever
I can't believe it.

Mr. Walter Dean Myers
is really really really
coming
to our school?

He was coming
to our city
anyway
to see his old buddy?

And he would be
honored
to visit
our clean school
and meet the mostly nice kids
who like his poems?

We sure are lucky
that his old buddy
lives in our town.

WOW!!!

MAY 28

The bulletin board
looks like it's
blooming words
with everybody's poems
up there
on all those
colored sheets of paper
yellow blue pink red green.

And the bookcase
looks like it's
sprouting books
all of them by
Mr. Walter Dean Myers
lined up
looking back at us
waiting for
Mr. Walter Dean Myers
himself

to come
to our school
right into our classroom.

Wow!

MAY 29

I can't wait.
I can't sleep.

Are you sure
you hid my poem
that was inspired
by Mr. Walter Dean Myers?

I don't want to do
any any anything
to upset him.

JUNE 1

MR.

    WALTER

        DEAN

            MYERS

                DAY

I NEVER
in my whole life
EVER
heard anybody
who could talk
like that
Mr. Walter Dean Myers.

All of my blood
in my veins
was bubbling
and all of the thoughts
in my head
were buzzing
and
I wanted to keep
Mr. Walter Dean Myers
at our school
forever.

JUNE 6

Dear Mr. Walter Dean Myers,

Thank you
a hundred million times
for
leaving your work
and your family
and your things-people-have-to-do
to come and visit us
in our school
in our class.

We hope you liked your visit.
We think maybe you did
because
you were
smile-smile-smiling
all over the place.

And when you read
your poems
you had the
best best BEST
voice
low and deep and friendly and warm
like it was reaching out and
wrapping us all up
in a big squeeze
and when you laughed
you had the
best best BEST
laugh I've ever heard in my life
like it was coming from way down deep
and bubbling up and
rolling and tumbling
out into the air.

We hope we didn't ask you
too many questions
but we thank you
for answering every which one
and especially for saying
that you would be
flattered
if someone used
some of your words
and especially if they
added a note that
they were
inspired by
Walter Dean Myers.

And it was nice of you
to read all of our poems
on the bulletin board
and I hope it didn't
make you
too sad
when you read the one

about my dog Sky
getting smooshed in the road.
And I think you liked
the brownies, too,
right?

Thank you for
coming to see us
Mr. Walter Dean Myers.

Inside this envelope
is a poem
using some of your words.
I wrote it.
It was
inspired by
you
Mr. Walter Dean Myers.

From your number one fan,

Jack

LOVE THAT DOG
(INSPIRED BY WALTER DEAN MYERS)
BY JACK

Love that dog,
like a bird loves to fly
I said I love that dog
like a bird loves to fly
Love to call him in the morning
love to call him
"Hey there, Sky!"

SOME OF THE POEMS USED
BY MISS STRETCHBERRY

The Red Wheelbarrow

BY WILLIAM CARLOS WILLIAMS

so much depends
upon

a red wheel
barrow

glazed with rain
water

beside the white
chickens.

Stopping by Woods on a Snowy Evening

BY ROBERT FROST

Whose woods these are I think I know.
His house is in the village, though;
He will not see me stopping here
To watch his woods fill up with snow.

My little horse must think it queer
To stop without a farmhouse near
Between the woods and frozen lake
The darkest evening of the year.

He gives his harness bells a shake
To ask if there is some mistake.
The only other sound's the sweep
Of easy wind and downy flake.

The woods are lovely, dark, and deep,
But I have promises to keep,
And miles to go before I sleep,
And miles to go before I sleep.

The Tiger*

BY WILLIAM BLAKE

Tiger! Tiger! burning bright
In the forests of the night,
What immortal hand or eye
Could frame thy fearful symmetry?

*First stanza

dog

BY VALERIE WORTH

Under a maple tree
The dog lies down,
Lolls his limp
Tongue, yawns,
Rests his long chin
Carefully between
Front paws;
Looks up, alert;
Chops, with heavy
Jaws, at a slow fly,
Blinks, rolls
On his side,
Sighs, closes
His eyes: sleeps
All afternoon
In his loose skin.

The Pasture

BY ROBERT FROST

I'm going out to clean the pasture spring;
I'll only stop to rake the leaves away
(And wait to watch the water clear, I may):
I shan't be gone long.—You come too.

I'm going out to fetch the little calf
That's standing by the mother. It's so young
It totters when she licks it with her tongue.
I shan't be gone long.—You come too.

Street Music

BY ARNOLD ADOFF

This city:
the
always
  noise
grinding
up from the
subways
under
  ground:
slamming from bus tires
and taxi horns and engines
of cars and trucks in all

vocabularies
                              of
clash
flash
screeching
hot metal language
  combinations:

as p l a n e s
 o v e r h e a d
            r o a r
a n
o r c h e s t r a
of rolling drums
and battle blasts
assaulting
            my ears
w i t h
t h e
a l w a y s
  n o i s e   o f
t h i s   c i t y :

street   music.

The Apple

BY S. C. RIGG

```
                              s
                            t
                          e
                        m

           apple  apple        apple apple
         apple yum apple   yum   apple yum apple
        juicy juicy juicy juicy juicy juicy juicy juicy juicy
       crunchy crunchy crunchy crunchy crunchy crunchy
      red yellow green red yellow green red yellow green red
    apple apple apple apple apple apple apple apple apple apple
    apple  apple apple apple apple apple apple apple apple  apple
    apple  apple apple apple apple  apple apple apple apple  apple
    yum delicious  yum delicious yum delicious yum delicious  yum
  yum yum yum yum yum yum yum yum yum yum yum yum yum yum
  yum yum yum yum yum yum yum yum yum yum yum yum yum yum
  yum yum yum yum yum yum yum yum yum yum yum yum yum yum
   yum yum yum yum yum yum wormy worm yuk  yuk  yum yum
   yum yum yum yum yum yum wormy worm  yuk  yuk yum yum
    yum yum yum yum yum yum yum yum yum yum yum yum
      yum delicious yum delicious yum delicious yum delicious
       apple apple apple apple apple apple apple apple apple
        apple apple apple apple apple apple apple apple
         apple apple apple apple apple apple apple
           red yellow green red yellow green red
            crunchy crunchy crunchy crunchy
               juicy juicy juicy juicy
                  apple apple
```

Love That Boy*

BY WALTER DEAN MYERS

Love that boy,
like a rabbit loves to run
I said I love that boy
like a rabbit loves to run
Love to call him in the morning
love to call him
"Hey there, son!"

*First stanza

Literature Circle Questions

Use the questions and activities that follow to get more out of the experience of reading *Love That Dog* by Sharon Creech.

1. Jack doesn't want to write poetry at the beginning of the book. Why doesn't he want to?

2. In Jack's first poem, he writes:

So much depends
upon
a blue car
splattered with mud
speeding down the road.

Why is the blue car important to Jack?

3. What causes Miss Stretchberry to be so interested in Jack's first poem? Describe what Miss Stretchberry does to get Jack to write more poems, especially about the blue car.

4. How does Jack respond when Miss Stretchberry asks him to write about a pet? Why do you think Miss Stretchberry encourages Jack to write the poem, despite his reaction?

5. What are Jack's feelings toward Sky? Make a list of details from the book that describe Jack's feelings toward his dog.

Note: The following questions are keyed to Bloom's taxonomy as follows: Knowledge: 1-3; Comprehension: 4-6; Application: 7-8; Analysis: 9-11; Synthesis: 12-13; Evaluation: 14-15.

6. Jack changes a great deal in the novel. Think about these changes. Then create a chart with two headings: "Beginning of school year" and "End of school year". Under each heading, list examples of the things Jack does, thinks, and says in the beginning of the year compared to the end of the year.

7. Imagine Miss Stretchberry has just asked Jack to write an essay telling what he has discovered about poetry and how it can change a person's life. What would the essay say?

8. Sky's death affected Jack deeply. If you had just lost a much-loved pet, what things could you or other people do to help you cope with the loss? Create a list of ideas.

9. Miss Stretchberry is able to convince Jack to write poetry and share his feelings even though he doesn't want to. Point out the qualities Miss Stretchberry has as a person and as a teacher that allow her to reach Jack.

10. Why does Jack fall in love with Walter Dean Myers's poetry? What effect does Mr. Myers's visit to the school have on Jack? How do you know?

11. There are many ways a poet can use words to paint a picture in a reader's mind. These devices include similes, metaphors, ono-matopoeia, and more. Find examples of the techniques the poets use in *Love That Dog*. As a group, choose three verses from the novel that created the most vivid pictures.

12. Did reading *Love That Dog* change your point of view about poetry? In what ways? Explain your answer.

13. At the end of the book, the author includes poems by seven famous American poets. Which poem did you like best, and why?

Activities

It's the end of the school year, and Jack wants to thank Miss Stretchberry for being such a great teacher. Compose a letter or write a poem from Jack that shows his appreciation for Miss Stretchberry.

Choose your favorite poem at the end of *Love That Dog*, and in your own words, explain what the narrator is trying to say.

In "The Apple", by S. C. Rigg, and "My Yellow Dog", by Jack, the words form the shape of the poem's subject. Write your own "shape" poem.

Get a collection of poems by your favorite poet. Read the collection, then select your favorite poem. Create a collage that illustrates what the poem is about.